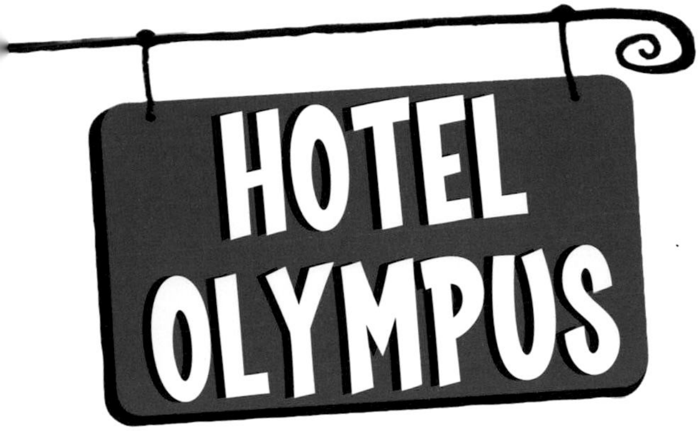
HOTEL
OLYMPUS

Published in 2010 by Windmill Books, LLC
303 Park Avenue South, Suite # 1280, New York, NY 10010-3657

Copyright © 2008, Edizioni EL S.r.l., Trieste Italy
Adaptations to North American Edition © 2010 Windmill Books

CREDITS:
Written by Sabina Colloredo
Illustrated by Antongionata Ferrari

Publisher Cataloging In Publication

Colloredo, Sabina, 1957-
          Hercules. – North American ed. / text by Sabina Colloredo ;
illustrated by Antongionata Ferrari.
          p.   cm. – (Hotel Olympus)
Summary: This is a retelling of Greek myths involving the heroic
Hercules, son of the god Zeus and the mortal Alcmene.
ISBN 978-1-60754-708-2
1. Heracles (Greek mythology)—Juvenile literature   2. Hercules (Roman
mythology)—Juvenile literature   3. Mythology, Greek—Juvenile literature
[1. Heracles (Greek mythology)   2. Hercules (Roman mythology)   3.
Mythology, Greek]   I. Ferrari, Antongionata   II. Title   III. Series
398.2/0938/02—dc22

Manufactured in the United States of America

CPSIA Compliance Information: Batch #BW10W: For further information contact Windmill Books, New York, New York at 1-866-478-0556.

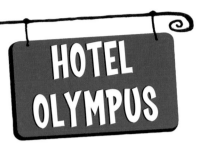

HERCULES

Text by Sabina Colloredo
Illustrated by Antongionata Ferrari

Skyview
Books™

an imprint of
WINDMILL BOOKS™
New York

CONTENTS

FLASH-FORWARD

Aphrodite lifted her skirt so she could run faster. She was bursting with great news for the gods of Mount Olympus.

"Zeus! Hera! Athena!" she screamed excitedly. "He's coming! He's coming!"

"Are you sure?" asked Hermes, the messenger of the gods.

Aphrodite nodded. "Look at that light in the distance…"

MANY YEARS BEFORE

The princess Alcmene was looking out the window of the palace and watched the city of Thebes lying at her feet. The streets were swarming with people hurrying toward their homes. Mothers held children by the hand, and looked at the sky with fear. A storm was coming. A rough wind blew in from the sea and heavy clouds darkened the late autumn day.

Alcmene leaned over the windowsill and looked toward the plain. Her husband was due to arrive any minute, but the road that ran along the wall was deserted. No sights or sounds hinted at the arrival of the commander

Amphitryon and his army. No messenger announced their arrival. A flash of lightning ripped the velvet gray sky. Alcmene was startled and jumped to her feet. At that moment, her door swung open and slammed against the wall.

"Who? What?" Alcmene stammered, terrified. Her husband Amphitryon, had appeared in the doorway.

"It's your husband!" he exclaimed, rushing to her. "Tired and hungry, but still alive and kicking." Alcmene was still startled, and felt a strange uneasiness. She studied her husband carefully. He looked the same as always, with his blond beard, square jaw, and skin that smelled of the wind and distant paths he had crossed. But there was something strange about him somehow. Something…different. She couldn't place it, but she sensed a powerful and mysterious force was behind it.

"Why are you staring at me?" snapped Amphitryon. "Aren't you glad to see me?"

Alcmene blushed. "Of course, I am happy… It's just strange to see you after all this time apart."

"I have been gone at war for a year. I should get a warmer welcome than this." As he spoke, thunder shook the building and the sky burst open, drenching the city. Alcmene rushed into his arms. "You are a grown woman, but you are still afraid of storms," he whispered gently. "But you must not fear the wrath of Zeus when I'm here to protect you." A burst of lightning lit up the sky, but Alcmene did not notice. She felt safe. It seemed like she was being lifted from the ground and placed on a cloud.

A LONG NIGHT

Hermes felt like he was flying blind in the pitch darkness of the storm. He and Helios, the Sun god, zigzagged across clouds that were spilling hail and rain. Rough air currents pushed them from all directions. Then Hermes took a deep breath and dove into a soft white cloud. When he came out, he was surrounded by blue sky. "I finally see sunlight," he exclaimed.

Helios, standing on his fiery chariot, looked at Hermes scornfully. "Who do you see, Hermes? What urgent message do you have for me?"

The messenger of the gods pointed to the thick clouds that hid the Earth. "I saw them! I bet Zeus is behind this storm," Hermes said. Hermes twirled and landed with his feet together on the backs of the winged horses that pulled Helios's chariot. "Oops!" Hermes exclaimed with a laugh. The horses started pawing nervously.

"Get down from there at once, fool! You're scaring the horses," yelled Helios. "So what's going on? Is this about Zeus?"

"Looks like our beloved king is hiding his latest romance with a nice storm. This time the lucky lady is Alcmene. She is a beauty and, as usual, Zeus can't help himself."

"Stop chattering, and tell me what I am supposed to do."

"Zeus commanded you to stop the chariot of the Sun," Hermes declared.

"What?!" Helios asked in disbelief.

"He wants a night that lasts three days for his new romance. Alcmene will become mother to an infant named Hercules. He'll become the greatest hero that ever Earth has ever known."

Helios became even angrier. "It is an impossible request! Men and nature need the Sun. Not even Zeus can stop the time!"

"It won't feel long to the world. Nobody will notice. They will just think they slept a little longer than usual and will wake up extra hungry. And you can take a little break yourself.

Anyway, you don't have a choice. You don't want to disobey the orders of the Chief. Do you want to be struck down by one of his lightning bolts?" Hermes asked the Helios, whose eyes were still flashing wildly.

Together with Apollo and Eros, Helios was one of the most beautiful gods of Olympus. Many goddesses were charmed by his winning smile. Hermes, on the other hand, was not handsome, but he had his own gifts. His craftiness and intelligence were the reasons Zeus trusted him to solve important problems.

"I'm going to the leave the Moon and all will be good and quite for three days." Helios finally agreed.

Hermes put on his helmet, preparing to leave.

"What about the queen?" asked Helios.

"Hera? She'll sleep like all the others," Hermes said simply.

"She won't sleep too long," Helios said. "She will figure out something's wrong."

AN ANGRY GUEST

Zeus raised his cup and all the gods seated at the banquet table did the same. He spoke with a thundering voice. "I propose a toast to the health of my last mortal son. The princess Alcmene will give birth to him today!" Glasses clinked, while many small lightning bolts lit up the sky. Zeus was beaming.

"I've never seen him so happy," Apollo whispered to his sister Artemis.

"He is madly in love with Alcmene," murmured Aphrodite.

"My son will be named Hercules," continued Zeus. "He will be the strongest and most just of men and will rule over the mortals."

"Oh, really?" a voice asked sharply. Everyone fell silent. Hera, the queen of the gods, was moving toward the throne, angrily pushing aside the clouds that floated in the great hall.

Zeus sprang to his feet. "Hera, I thought you were in the garden of the Hesperides!"

"I got bored and lonely out there, so I decided to come home early." Her green eyes darted everywhere and no one dared breathe. The queen was famous for her rages throughout all Olympus. "I see that I was right to return. I don't like to miss festivities, or births, or weddings."

She sat on the throne of clouds with her husband. "Stop staring at me with that stunned look. Don't let me spoil the party." In a quieter voice, Hera whispered to her husband. "I cannot believe that you have betrayed me again! You will pay for this."

"You know I love only you. It was a silly romance. Please do not make a scene," Zeus begged.

"And this Hercules? When he is born, what will be his position among your children? I want you to make a vow right now that our children will always be the most powerful," Hera insisted.

"What are they saying?" asked Athena. The gods tried to listen in, but they could not hear what was being said.

"Promise me," Hera said. Hera wanted her offspring to rule over all others. Zeus toyed with an arrow to buy time.

"Do you want me to scream?" Hera asked impatiently.

"Okay, I swear," Zeus sighed.

Hera stood up. "All right, dear. You've made the right choice." Hera gave him a quick kiss on the forehead and stormed out of the hall.

BROTHERS BY BLOOD

Hebe and Eileithyia were listening to their brother Ares talk about his latest battle. "…So I ripped apart the back of the dragon with a sword, and the enemy army and its commander slid off the monster's back and were destroyed!"

"Stop, Ares. You're going to scare your sisters." Hera had come into the room in a fury. "You kids knew about Alcmene and did not tell me. What kind of children are you? I can't trust anyone."

Hebe, the goddess of youth, embraced her gently. "Please, Mother, don't be so angry. We only wanted to protect you. We knew that you were on vacation and didn't want to upset you."

"Maybe it's not too late to fix this mess! Eileithyia, you're the goddess of childbirth. You will go to Alcmene and make sure she stays in labor for a long time. At same time, I'll go to Queen Nicippe of Mycenae. She is seven months pregnant. I will make sure her son is born before Hercules is born."

"N-no, Mother, I can't interfere," stammered Eileithyia.

"You can and you will," Hera demanded. "Your brother Ares has taught you that in love and war you have to do what you need to do to win. Right, Ares?"

"Sure, yes," Ares, the god of war, agreed, "but I do not quite understand the plan. What does Nicippe's future son have to do with Hercules?"

"Use your brain, Ares," sighed Hera. Ares was her favorite son, but he wasn't terribly bright. "Nicippe is a descendant of Perseus, one of the many illegitimate children of Zeus. Her child will be a descendant of Zeus, too. This child will be named Eurystheus. He will have your father's blood in him. If Eurystheus is born first, he will have the right to reign, and Hercules will be a nobody. Do you understand now?"

Hera turned to Eileithyia. "Fly now. And do your duty!"

THE LITTLE BIG MAN

The Sun had just set and the palace of Thebes, where Alcmene and Amphitryon lived, was filled with a dim blue light. Alcmene loved this time of day: Her twins, Hercules and Iphicles, were fed and clean and ready to sleep. She could have a little time to herself before going to bed. She looked lovingly at her children, who were sleeping close to each other in the cradle.

Although he was only ten months, Hercules was more than twice the size of other babies his age, including his brother. He was a true giant, with a head of blond curls and a strong body.

Alcmene looked at him tenderly and kissed him. He was strong and brave, and yet it was the weak Eurystheus who would reign in his place. Hera had made sure of that. Alcmene sighed, but the Gods could decide how things would go for the mortals.

Alcmene kissed her other son, Iphicles, rocked the cradle gently, and left the room. As she walked along the hallway that led to her room, the building was silent except for the sound of her footsteps. In the quiet, she tried to imagine what the future held for her twins. As happened every time, she had a premonition. In this vision of the future, she saw the face of Hercules as an adult. He was exhausted and in pain. She shuddered.

Hercules was the son of Zeus. Iphicles was the son of her husband Amphitryon. She loved them both with all her heart, but she worried more about Hercules. She feared her husband's anger if

23

he found out the truth. But it was not her fault. Zeus had pretended to be her husband when they had their romance. The only thing that mattered now was that she would protect her son. She would fight for him even if that meant she had to stand up to the most powerful of the goddesses.

HERA'S ASSASSINS

At midnight two snakes covered with purple scales slithered across the sleeping city of Thebes. The gate of Amphitryon's palace opened silently in front of them and the serpents slithered toward the nursery. They found the two sleeping babies. Their forked tongues were ready to strike. Suddenly, Iphicles awoke. When he saw the snakes, he let out a piercing shriek. He kicked so hard in fear that the cradle overturned.

In her bedroom, on the other side of the building, Alcmene sat bolt upright in bed.

"Iphicles! Hercules!" she screamed. "Wake up, Amphitryon!" Without waiting for her husband, she jumped out of bed and headed for the nursery.

Her husband pulled the sword from the wall and followed his wife.

"Alcmene! What is happening?"

"Run! Can't you hear the screaming? The children are in danger!"

Amphitryon rushed forward, calling the palace guards to help him. Alcmene tried to keep up, but her husband ran faster. She found herself alone in the maze of hallways. Then she heard an evil laugh. "Hera, is that you? You are a mother, too. I beg you, please do not hurt my children." But it was Hercules who saved the day.

When Iphicles saw the snakes and screamed, Hercules awoke with a start. He felt a cold drop of poison on his forehead and jumped up. He found something soft and pressed with his fingers of steel. He was mad because those things slithering in the darkness had scared his little brother. He crushed the snakes in his hands until the monsters were dead, with their tongues hanging out of their mouths. At that moment, Amphitryon, the guards, the nurse, and Alcmene burst into the room. Hercules proudly showed off the two dead snakes. Iphicles was sitting on the floor, confused, but safe.

"Iphicles!" shouted Alcmene, lifting him from the ground and kissing him. kisses. You are safe."

"Hercules!" Amphitryon exclaimed, taking him in his arms and holding up in front of everyone. "Look at him! He has the courage and the strength of a god!"

When the room was quiet again, Alcmene wrapped Hercules in a blanket and rocked him gently. "Become a powerful warrior and, when you grow up, win back the throne that belongs to you," she whispered. But Hercules was already asleep.

A PLAN

"Trust me!" Hermes repeated impatiently. "And do what I say."

Alcmene looked worried. "I wish Zeus had come here himself. I'm not sure this is a good plan."

"Zeus has more important things to do!" Hermes shot back. "Now, there's no time to lose."

Alcmene held Hercules tightly in her arms. "Don't worry," she whispered, "your mother is here." She looked at him with love. Can you say 'mama'?

"Mammmmmm-a!" Hercules yelped.

"Shush!" Hermes scolded. "Do you want to be discovered?"

Alcmene shot him an angry look. "This is easy for you. He's not your son. You don't have to worry about some awful beast hurting this small, helpless child."

"Helpless? This child killed two snakes with his bare hands!"

"Never mind," Alcmene said, "I can't help being worried. If anything happens to him, I will never forgive myself. I'm not going back to Thebes. I am going to hide among those olive trees and wait in case my son needs me.

The messenger of the gods looked up to the heavens. "What should I do with her, Zeus?" Lightning streaked across the blue sky.

Hermes understood the message. "Okay, okay. I'll make sure she gets to the trees safely." He led Alcmene to a hiding place among the trees. Alcmene gave a last kiss to Hercules, then watched Hermes fly away with her precious son.

A DROP OF MILK

Helios was riding his fiery chariot over the tops of the mountains, when Hera and Athena stepped out from a bend in the path. As usual, the two strong-willed goddesses were arguing heatedly.

"Your father cannot continue to betray me in this way," Hera was saying. "I'm out of patience. Alcmene must be the last, or I will move to the garden of the Hesperides for good." Suddenly, she stopped and raised her head, listening. "Did you hear something, Athena? Did you hear a crying sound?"

Ignoring the thorns, she pushed into the bushes. "Look!" Hera exclaimed. She was holding Hercules in her arms. The huge baby was kicking wildly. "What a big baby!" Hera said. "How could a mother leave her child out here alone?"

"Perhaps there is a reason," Athena muttered, looking down. She had agreed to be part of the plan Zeus and Hermes had come up with, but she did not like lying to others. She hoped it would all be over soon.

Hercules continued to kick and squirm. "What a strong child. I would be proud of a son like this. I could never leave him. But human beings are so wild. But this is a beautiful baby. These violet eyes look like Zeus's."

Athena got nervous when Hera spoke of Zeus.

"And look at his strong muscles. You remind me so much of my own son Ares! This baby must be very hungry! He needs some mother's milk. Hera fed the baby with her own milk. Some of the milk splashed into the sky.

Athena watched the droplets of milk fill the sky and form a new galaxy. "This galaxy should be called the Milky Way," Athena said in amazement.

But Hera was tired now. "Take this baby. He is so strong, he is hurting me. It's always the same. Try to do good to mortals and we get nothing but trouble." Hera flew off.

When Hera had disappeared on her golden chariot, Athena let out her battle cry. Hearing the cry, two shadows came out from among the trees: Alcmene and Hermes.

"Hera has nursed Hercules. Now your son has the strength he will need to face what lies ahead," said the goddess, putting Hercules into Alcmene's waiting arms. "When he is grown, Eurystheus will set great challenges for Hercules. They would be impossible for any human being." Alcmene paled.

"Go on, Athena," Hermes said. "You're frightening her to death."

"But he is not any human being. And if he passes all the tests, he will have a great prize," finished Athena.

"What kind of prize?" Alcmene asked quietly.

"Zeus will tell you in time. And now, farewell, Princess!" Alcmene bowed to the ground. She had to turn her eyes away from Athena. The goddess was so beautiful and bright, it hurt to look at her for too long. When Alcmene raised her eyes, she was alone in the darkness of the night, with Hercules in her arms.

TWINS

Hera's milk was very strong. At eight years old, Hercules was already taller and stronger than a grown man. He could drive a chariot better than his father. Amphitryon found the best teachers to train his son. He even asked Gods to teach Hercules skills like sword fighting and archery. At fourteen, Hercules had won many fights.

Zeus became more and more proud of Hercules as he grew into a young man.. He gave him a gold shield carved with snake heads to scare away enemies. Hercules showed a tough face to the world, but one person knew even the great hero had doubts and worries: his twin brother.

"I've missed you, brother," Hercules mumbled with his mouth full. Iphicles had welcomed his brother with a magnificent fireside feast. "All my favorite foods," Hercules sighed with contentment. Iphicles had waited patiently, but finally burst out.

"Come on now, brother, stop stuffing your face, and tell me some battle stories. It is true that you have fought enemies so fierce that they eat their own dead soldiers in battle?"

Hercules carefully studied his brother's face, which was now covered with a bushy black beard. "Tell me about yourself instead. It's been years since we've seen each other. Your son Iolaus is a smart boy. You're a lucky man."

"Look who's talking," Iphicles laughed. "You're the hero of heroes."

"Do not say that," Hercules said. "You have things I do not have."

"I have a family, it is true, but you're everything that every man wants to be."

Hercules stared into the distance, beyond the open window, beyond the quietly falling snow. It was the usual story. Everyone wanted to be him, but who did he want to be?

"I'm good at killing and nothing else. Before I was even born, someone else decided that's what I would be."

"Why are you complaining? What would you do if you weren't a warrior?"

"Farm the land, get married, have children, build cities, go to sea. There are so many things I could do."

"You can say that because you're already a hero," Iphicles said.

"But I have no choice," said Hercules. "If I did, I'd be an ordinary man. This is the difference between being the son of a god and being the son of a mortal. But never mind, brother." Hercules gave Iphicles a pat on the back. He forgot his own strength, so the pat knocked Iphicles to the ground.

"Ouch!" Iphicles exclaimed, rubbing his head.

"Serves you right, brother. You do not appreciate what you have. Our father Amphitryon is not a killing machine, but he is a great captain!" Iphicles did not dare argue. When Hercules's eyes turned icy blue, it even made his twin brother shiver. Iphicles knew his brother had a temper. He could go from happiness to anger in seconds. Better not to make him angry.

Hercules blew out the candle flame and the room was only the soft light of the embers. "Let us go to sleep now. Tomorrow I have to go to Argos. King Eurystheus has called me to his court." The two brothers stretched out on the rug beside the fire, just as they had done when they were little.

"What does he want from you? Be careful of him. He's jealous of your fame," warned Iphicles.

"I think the time has come at last," Hercules said. "After all these years of fighting and training, Eurystheus is going to test me. If I pass these tests, there will be a great prize. I do not know what it will be, but I believe it will be worth the effort.

"Maybe it will be glory, fame, immortality…" Iphicles said. Hercules heard a note of jealousy in his brothers' voice. This hurt him deeply. This happened with many friends, teachers, and even in romances. When people saw how much faster and stronger Hercules was at everything, they pulled away from him. Hercules watched his brother's sleeping form. He did not want to lose his brother's love, too. They had never been jealous of each other. Iphicles was intelligent and thoughtful, while Hercules was strong and quick to act, but they had always gotten along. Hercules did not want things to change. He lay awake until dawn.

THE KING'S ORDER

Hercules felt uncomfortable in the throne room, which was filled with people. There was a mixture of fear and excitement in the air. He missed his tent, which was the only home he had. He liked how the fresh air could get into it. Hercules approached the throne and stared straight at Eurystheus.

"So here is the big hero!" hissed the king. "I look forward to seeing you at work!"

"I await your orders," said Hercules.

"Your first job, or labor, will be to kill the lion of Nemea and bring me his fur."

"They say that no weapon can hurt him," said Hercules.

"Exactly. Not iron, wood, or stone can hurt him. That monster is the son of the underworld." The king laughed loudly, but the rest of the room was quiet. The people were all on Hercules's

side. And they knew the Nemean Lion was a horrible beast that had eaten men, women, and children.

"But you have nothing to fear, right? If you are the son of Zeus, as people say, then your Daddy will help you in time."

This angered Hercules. He shouted at the king. "Come down from that throne. Give me your ring. That is my throne!"

The king called his guards to protect him. "Settle down, Hercules. You know you have no choice but to obey me."

Hercules grabbed a club and was about to leap at the wall of soldiers protecting the king, when he heard a voice in his ear.

"Stop. What are you doing?" He recognized the voice of the goddess Athena. "This is not your destiny. Eurystheus and his tests are part of a bigger plan for you. There is a bigger prize." Thunder exploded in the sky. Hercules picked up his club and left the palace. The bright afternoon sunlight made him squint. He started walking down the dusty road. He had to face what was ahead.

THE FIRST LABOR

Mount Treto, where the lion of Nemea lived, was deserted. A single trail led to the top. There were bones along the trail—bones of people and animals the lion had killed. Hercules listened for any sound as he climbed. It had been almost two days since he had seen another person. There were just some empty farms and fields. A shepherd warned Hercules that he was in the land of the monster. Everyone else had run away or been eaten by the beast. But Hercules continued to climb. When he reached the top, he kept his club in his hands. As he waited for the beast, he thought of his kind mother Alcmene.

"Do not worry, Mother," he whispered, "you will be proud of me."

Hercules waited outside the entrance to the cave, hidden among the brush. He waited for a very long time. Finally, as the Sun was going down, the lion appeared on top of the path. The beast looked like a creature of the underworld. He looked like a big bull with shaggy black fur. He had long sharp tusks that reached from his jaws to the ground. When he got near the cave, he stopped and sniffed the air. Hercules wasted no time.

"Father, protect me!" Hercules shouted as he leapt out of the bushes with his club tightly in his hands. Two yellow eyes, surrounded by a thick mane, stared at him in surprise. Man and beast stared at each other, then the lion jumped.

Hercules threw himself sideways and hit the lion hard on the head. The crash was terrible, but the lion just shook his mane. Then Hercules remembered Eurystheus's warning--that no weapon of wood or stone would kill the beast.

Then he remembered Athena's wisdom. "Use only weapons that you carry with you." And when the lion stood up for a second jump, Hercules reached out his hands abruptly, as he had done many years ago with the snakes. He grabbed the lion's neck and squeezed. Man and beast rolled together in the dust. As they struggled, Hercules thought about his childhood and his many battles. He closed his eyes and squeezed the lion's neck even more tightly. He only let go when the lion's head was hanging in his hands. It was over. He had killed the lion.

The people were safe again. The monster wouldn't threaten them anymore. Hercules sat down and looked up at the blue sky. A flash of lightning lit up the sky. Zeus was proud of him.

51

"Did you see that, Zeus?" Hercules cried out. "I've done it!" The story of how Hercules killer the Nemean Lion passed from person to person all across Greece. Soon, everyone knew about Hercules and the feat he had accomplished.

HERA'S PLAN

Hera walked among the clouds that floated through the palace. She picked a small, puffy cloud and put it on her throne. "Come sit by me, Ares. This cloud is very soft!"

"I don't care about clouds," Ares shouted. "Mother, on the Earth they say that Hercules is stronger than me. You must do something!"

"Yes, Ares, he killed a lion and has won some battles! But why do you worry so much, dear? He's just a man. In a few years, he will be dead and buried and nobody will remember him. Humans forget so fast!"

"Maybe so, mother. But for now, all of Greece is talking about him. And the women love him, too," added Aphrodite. Her beautiful eyes changed color with her moods. Right now, they were the color of a golden sunset.

"Never mind that, Aphrodite. I'm worried about Ares." She looked at her strong, but frustrated son. "Do not worry, Ares. There is always a solution. Someone must give Eurystheus an idea for a harder test. Athena will help Hercules, but if the task is too dangerous, even she won't be able to save him. "And Ares, you mustn't hold onto my skirts like a child. That does not make you seem strong!"

"Yes, Mother, but tell me what you have in mind. I can see from the light in your eye that you have an idea."

"Just promise not to talk to your father." Then she stood on tiptoe and began whispering in her son's ear: "Do you remember that monster that lives in the swamp of Lerna? It is called the Hydra, I think…"

THE SECOND LABOR

The swamp of Lerna was as big as the sea. It was yellow and smelly, and it always covered in fog. Hercules caught up with the war chariot driven by his nephew Iolaus, the son of Iphicles, who had wanted to help his uncle. When they stopped near the Hydra's den, the horses whinnied in fear. The air felt heavy and damp.

"This place gives me the chills," Iolaus exclaimed, jumping off the chariot. Is it true that the Hydra has seven snake heads and the body of a dog?"

"Those who have seen it have not lived to tell. But soon we'll see for ourselves." Hercules looked at his nephew. He was proud and thankful for his help, but he did not want him to take foolish risks. "Iolaus, whatever happens, stay behind me, all right?"

"Do not worry, Uncle."

"Hera has ordered the Hydra to kill me. The Hydra is even more dangerous than the lion I fought. One of the Hydra's heads is immortal. If I can separate that head from the body, I can defeat the Hydra. But if something goes wrong, you know what to do."

"Jump on the chariot and go home," repeated Iolaus, but he did not sound like he meant it.

"Do not say it like that. Do not be ashamed to protect yourself," Hercules told his nephew.

Now they had to concentrate on killing the
Hydra and bringing one head back to
Eurystheus. Suddenly, they saw a child
struggling in the middle of the swamp. The
Hydra had dragged the child off a wagon. The
muddy water was still for a moment, then there
was a rush of water and a muffled cry from the
swamp. Hercules stood with his legs wide apart
for balance. He held his sword in one hand. He
had used a piece of cloth to cover his mouth to
protect him from the monster's poisonous
breath. He didn't have to wait long. Suddenly,
the Hydra surfaced.

"There are ten heads!" Hercules shouted,
pointing to the snake heads that were biting the
child who had been pulled into the swamp.
Suddenly, the Hydra was coming toward
Hercules.

"Stay back, Iolaus!" With a single stroke of
the sword, Hercules cut off two heads that rose
toward them.

"By Zeus," shouted Iolaus. "Uncle, look!" The Hydra grew two new heads to replace the ones that had been cut off. Hercules was taken by surprise. That's why this monster is so powerful, he thought. It's almost immortal—it can't be killed, or can it?

THE CRAB

Hercules and Iolaus fought back to back for hours, trying to escape the heads of the Hydra and its poisonous breath. Hercules was worried about his nephew. Iolaus was exhausted and sweating, but still fighting. If anything happened to him, he would never forgive himself. His nephew, along with his mother and brother, were the most important things in the world to him. He prayed to Zeus to keep Iolaus safe.

"Please, Zeus, help Iolaus. He's young and innocent. He deserves to live a long life. Take my life if you want, but save his." Finishing his prayer, Hercules landed another blow. It cut off three heads, but Hercules knew more would grow back in their place. He didn't have time to notice that a giant swamp crab was crawling out of the mud.

"Uncle! Careful!" cried Iolaus. The crab was coming toward Hercules, with its great pincers raised.

"Leave him to me!" roared the hero. He crushed the crab under his heel. His blood was boiling, but he calmed down when he heard Athena's soft voice.

"Use the flames," suggested Athena. "Fire destroys the Hydra, not the sword." Hercules acted quickly.

"Iolaus! Light fire to a stick and bring it to me!"

Iolaus lit a stick and brought it to his Uncle. The Hydra moved back in fear. Hercules knew the Hydra would be back, but now he knew the Hydra's weak spot.

"When I cut, you burn!" Hercules ordered his nephew. And that's how they beat the Hydra. Hercules cut off a head, then Iolaus burned the spot with fire. That way, a new head could not grow back. At sunset, the Hydra had only one head left. This head, covered in flakes of gold, was immortal. Hercules trapped the last head in a bronze container.

"I will bring this trophy back to Eurystheus," said Hercules, sealing the cap.

"It will prove we beat the Hydra, but it will frighten the king, too." Then he turned to his nephew and hugged him. "You were very brave."

Iolaus was too tired to answer. He was exhausted and ready to go home. The fog from the monster's poisonous breath was disappearing. For the first time in years, stars twinkled above the swamp.

"Watch, Iolaus. Life is returning to this place of death," Hercules said, as the horses broke into a trot. "Sometimes I think that the tests which Eurystheus is giving me are not just to help me earn a place among heroes. I think they are helping rid the Earth of evil creatures that haunt people and destroy land, monsters like the Hydra. What do you think?"

But his nephew did not answer. He had fallen asleep, lulled by the rocking of the chariot. It was a long trip home, but Hercules was filled with joy and pride.

BACK ON MOUNT OLYMPUS

"He crushed my favorite crab!" screamed Hera, while Zeus quietly polished his arrows.

"Well, my dear, have you not already rewarded the crab's bravery by turning him into the constellation Cancer?" asked Zeus calmly. Zeus always found it best to cool Hera's anger with soothing words. Sometimes it worked.

Now Hera directed her anger at Athena, who was deep in conversation with Hermes. "And you—don't you interfere again. Understand? Or I'll…"

Hera lost her train of thought. Zeus had wrapped his big arms around Hera and was stroking her hair. "Aw, you're so beautiful when you're angry," he said. This technique—flattery—always worked.

"Oh, stop it, Zeus. You know I can't stay angry when you do that," coocd Hera. Athena and Hermes quietly left the room.

"I have no weapons against you, you know," said Hera.

"I know. Thank the gods!" chuckled Zeus.

All of Mount Olympus seemed to sigh with relief. There was peace among the gods. At least for now.

THE THIRD LABOR

The golden head of the Hydra made a fine trophy to bring back to Eurystheus. People from all over Greece came to marvel at the head, which was displayed in a special display case. The visitors all had the same name on their lips: Hercules.

Hercules's growing fame was driving Eurystheus crazy. He tried to come up with a third labor at which Hercules might fail—or better yet, meet his doom.

For his third labor, Hercules had to capture the Ceryneian Hind. The Ceryneian Hind was a large female deer that no hunter had been able to catch. It was said that it could outrun and arrow in flight.

The Ceryneian Hind was sacred to Artemis. Eurystheus hoped that this task would anger Artemis so that she would punish Hercules.

Hercules chased the Ceryneian Hind for a full year. He followed it through the forests throughout Greece. Then one morning, the beautiful beast lay down at Hercules's feet. Hercules looked into the Ceryneian Hind's eyes and was touched by its graceful beauty. He thought that only a man as cruel as Eurystheus would want to capture such a wonderful animal. His face lit up as an idea came to him. He made a vow to Artemis, gently picked up the Ceryneian Hind, and brought it to Argos.

The crowd swelled around Hercules and followed him to the palace. They could not believe he had captured the Ceryneian Hind.

He had completed the third of his impossible labors!

When Hercules reached the castle, he made sure that Eurystheus got a good long look at the Ceryneian Hind. Eurystheus grudgingly congratulated Hercules on completing the labor. He reached out toward the animal, and Hercules let go, fulfilling his vow to Artemis that he would release the Ceryneian Hind back to her.

"Guess you weren't quick enough," said Hercules as he exited the palace grounds.

THE NEXT FIVE LABORS

"What a softy—you let the hind go!" mocked Eurystheus.

Hercules looked at the king. Although his life had been far easier than Hercules's, the king looked older and more tired than the hero. If he hadn't been such a mean person, Hercules would have felt sorry for him.

Still, Eurystheus's desire to see Hercules fail was inexhaustible. He assigned Hercules his fourth labor: to capture the Erymanthian Boar. The Erymanthian Boar was a man-eating beast. Surely that beast would make a tidy meal of

Hercules. Hercules captured the beast, and when he brought it back to Eurystheus, the king cowered in fear of it and demanded that he release it. All in all, the fourth labor ended up being a humiliating affair for the king.

Eurystheus plotted to devise a fifth labor that would humiliate Hercules, rather than challenge his strength and add to his heroic fame. He assigned Hercules to clean the Augean stables in a single day. The Augean stables which housed divine cattle and horses. These immortal animals were known for creating...well, incredible amounts of manure. Eurystheus laughed to himself as he thought of Hercules waist-deep in manure. "Let him try to come out of this one smelling like a rose!" he thought.

Sure enough, Hercules did. He changed the course of two rivers, which washed the Augean stables clean.

73

Enraged, Eurystheus devised a sixth labor for Hercules. He would have to kill the man-eating Stymphalian birds. Athena supplied Hercules with magical castanets that made terrifying noise. Hercules used the castanets to scare the birds into flight, then shot them down with his arrows.

Eurystheus was sure Hercules would be defeated by the seventh labor. He had to capture the Cretan Bull. Hercules choked the bull with his bare hands and sent it—still alive—to the king. Eurystheus wanted to sacrifice the bull to Hera, but she refused it, because the gift would technically be from Hercules, not Eurystheus.

Eurystheus was sure he'd picked an impossible task for the eighth labor. Hercules was ordered to round up the Mares of Diomedes. These were four wild horses to which King Diomedes fed his enemies. Hercules fed the king to his own horses. Then he sewed their mouths shut and sent them to Eurystheus.

Eurystheus was exasperated by Hercules's success. He vowed that the next labor would be more dangerous than any that had come before...

THE NINTH LABOR

Hercules stood on the ship's deck, staring thoughtfully at the coast that was coming into view. He was headed to a wild and barren land. His ninth labor was to steal Hippolyta's girdle. Hippolyta was queen of the Amazons, a nation of women warriors. Her girdle was a sacred belt that her father, Ares, had given to her, and which she always wore.

Hercules thought of his family. His nephew Iolaus had become a valuable companion on his labors. Eurystheus had turned his brother against him; his talk had made Iphicles jealous of his brother, and resentful of Hercules's close relationship with Iolaus. The brothers had not spoken to each other in years.

Hercules drove these negative thoughts away. It was important for him to clear his head before taking on a challenge. Hippolyta was a legendary warrior. Hercules wondered how he should go about this labor. As a warrior, he was much more used to dealing with men than with women.

"There are three Amazonian queens, you say—sisters?" asked Hercules.

Iolaus nodded. "Yes: Hippolyta, Antiope, and Melanippe. Hippolyta leads them."

"Is she the most beautiful of the three?" interrupted Theseus.

"Her beauty is not what we're after, Theseus," said Hercules impatiently. "Tomorrow we will drop anchor."

"Our arrival won't go unnoticed," warned Iolaus. "Remember not to do anything foolish. The Amazons are great archers. One false move and they could easily take us down."

"But they're women!" scoffed Theseus.

"I'm more afraid of women than of men!" said Hercules. "Especially Amazons. They are trained from birth to kill men." He laughed nervously. The ship sank into an awkward silence.

"Never underestimate any opponent," advised Hercules.

QUEEN OF THE AMAZONS

Hippolyta appeared to Hercules as if in a vision. The wind gently lifted her long dark hair as she rode her horse toward the shore where the men had docked. Her helmet gleamed in the Sun. Hercules met eyes with her and his stomach did a little flip-flop. She turned her horse around and returned to the woods.

"See?" said Theseus, smiling. "Not bad, right?"

"Iolaus, bring the horses from the ship," ordered Hercules. Iolaus walked away to do as he had been told.

Hercules felt flushed. He was worried that he might be coming down with something. Theseus chuckled and said, "Ho-ho—I think you just came down with a little crush on the queen!" teased Theseus.

Hercules shuddered a bit without knowing why. He didn't see anything, but he could feel a hostile presence somewhere.

He didn't see that Hera was watching him from above. She was pleased with the way things were going. Eros, Aphrodite's son, had just shot Hercules with one of his invisible magic arrows that make their victims fall hopelessly in love.

"Oh, your heart is about to be broken just like Zeus broke mine with your mother!" whispered Hera fiercely.

HERCULES MEETS HIPPOLYTA

Hercules sent his warriors to spread out over the Amazon's lands.

"Look around. Talk to anyone you can—especially anyone who doesn't want to talk. That usually means they know something important," instructed Hercules. "I want to find out as much as I can about this place and about its queen." His men saluted him and took off into the woods.

Hercules remained on the deck of the ship, staring off into the distance. He sighed, thinking of Hippolyta's shiny hair.

At sunset one of his men came running back to the ship, shaking with fear. "Someone's here to see you," he stammered, looking pale.

Hercules could smell the wind in Hippolyta's hair before he could see her. She approached him from behind. Her girdle belted the waist of her bright red dress. The girdle was made of gold and encrusted with jewels that shone in the sunset.

"Hippolyta," Hercules exclaimed, bowing to her and blushing. "You should have told me you were coming. I would have prepared a feast worthy of you and your fellow warriors."

Hippolyta smiled. "I've come alone," she said. "So you are the famous Hercules?" She looked at him as confidently as a cat playing with a mouse. "Hercules, son of Zeus, the big hero, and so on?"

Hercules nodded and blushed.

"I find all of this talk of you annoying, frankly. Before you came along I was Hippolyta the Great, the Amazon that was the talk of the world."

"Sorry," muttered Hercules.

"So, tell me: Why are you here?"

Hercules stared at her, unable to come up with an answer. Usually he was quick-witted in these situations, full of ideas and plans. Now, however, he felt as if his mind was clouded over.

"Please, your Highness, I am at your disposal," was all he could think to say.

"I'm not interested in a servant," she shot back. She pointed a finger at his chest. "I have a better idea. I am the queen of the Amazons, the most powerful woman on Earth. You are Hercules, the strongest man on Earth. Do you see where I'm going with this? I want a daughter. A daughter by you would be a powerful woman indeed." She took him by the hand and led him back onto his ship.

Hera watched this scene from above. "It's all falling into place," she muttered.

Hera took the form of an Amazon warrior and descended to the ground. She jumped on a horse and rode back toward the city shouting: "Help! Hercules has kidnapped our queen!"

APHRODITE STEPS IN

Aphrodite laid on her shell near the shore and let the sound of the lapping waves soothe her. Nobody was calling her, nobody needed her. It was a rare moment. She fell into a gentle sleep with a smile on her lips.

"Auntie Aphrodite!" Hebe's sudden scream made Aphrodite leap to her feet. The shell she was sitting on tipped over and she fell into the water. When she emerged she was furious.

"How many times have I told you not to call me 'Auntie'?" she shouted at Hebe. "If you do it again, I swear I'll stab you with one of Eros's arrows!"

"That's exactly what I needed to talk to you about," said Hebe, trying to catch her breath.

"Well, what is it?" asked Aphrodite.

"It's about Hercules!" said Hebe. "I know everything. I know that Hera told you to send Eros to pierce Hercules's heart with an arrow. Now Hercules is at Hippolyta's mercy and she'll kill him once she gets what she wants from him. You have to stop this!"

"What does it matter to you, Hebe?"

Hebe looked down, blushing. "Hercules is a great man. He's a hero. It's not right to allow him to be killed on my mother's whim."

"Your mother is the queen of the gods. Her whims, as you call them, are orders." Aphrodite paused and studied Hebe carefully. "Oh—you're in love with Hercules!"

"Yes, I am," admitted Hebe. "Mother doesn't know. But I beg you: Don't tell her. I know she hates him. If she kills him, I couldn't bear it!"

"In this case," said Aphrodite, "your problem falls squarely into my realm. I can take care of this. First thing's first: Only Eros can withdraw his love spell, and he almost never does. But what son can say no to his mother, eh?"

HIPPOLYTA'S GIRDLE

Hercules sank into Hippolyta's embrace. He was overwhelmed by feelings of love unlike any he had ever felt before. He felt as though he couldn't live or breathe without her. Losing Hippolyta would be more painful than any defeat. He wanted to give up his labors and spend the rest of his life with her.

"Stay with me," he whispered, "or kill me."

Hippolyta found Hercules's sudden passion for her a bit much, but she figured maybe that was just the way with larger-than-life heroes. "Um, sure, we'll see," she said.

"Promise," he said. Hippolyta crossed her fingers behind her back. "I promise," she said.

Hercules felt a terrible pain near his heart. He groaned and put a hand to his chest. When he opened his eyes, the pain had disappeared, along with Eros's enchanted arrow.

He looked at Hippolyta as if for the first time. "What am I doing here? Where are my men?" he asked, leaping to his feet.

The queen looked at him, confused by his sudden mood change. Still, she couldn't help admiring his muscular body.

"You sent your men into town, remember?" Hippolyta reached for him, and he pushed her away. Hippolyta's confusion turned to anger. It

seemed like their friendly alliance would end in
a fight. She reached for her girdle, the golden
belt with jewels. Hercules grabbed her wrist.

"Where do you think you're going?" asked
Hercules, his anger rising. "Whatever spell
you put me under, I've overcome it. I'm taking
your golden girdle back home. You can come,
too. I'll sell you to the slave market for what
you've done!"

In his rage, Hercules had forgotten that Hippolyta was no ordinary woman, but a warrior like him. She freed herself from his grip, grabbed her golden belt, and raced up to the ship's deck. Hercules chased after her.

FIGHTING THE AMAZONS

Every street, every alley in the city raged with the battle between the Amazons and Hercules's men. There was no reason the two sides should be fighting, since Hercules had come in peace. It was only thanks to Hera spreading rumors and drumming up distrust of the men that this bloodshed came about.

The fighting continued for a long time. Hippolyta's face shone with sweat. Hercules could tell that her energy was fading, but despite that she continued to fight fiercely. He couldn't help but admire her: No other person had ever lasted so long in a fight against him. Something of Eros's arrow seemed to remain in his heart. He had felt relieved to allow himself to surrender to someone. He missed that feeling already, no matter how artificial it had been.

"Don't look at me like that!" cried Hippolyta, as if she could read his thoughts. She clanged her sword against his. Hercules thought he saw a tear in the corner of her eye. He blocked her next blow, knocking Hippolyta's sword from her hands. The queen was disarmed!

THE CHOICE

Hippolyta's cry swept away all other sound. It was a sound that her fellow warriors dreaded to hear: It meant that their queen was unarmed and at the mercy of the enemy.

The Amazons, sensing the battle was lost, stopped fighting. A deathly silence fell over the city. The only sounds were the water lapping the hull of the ship and Hercules's men returning to the port.

Hercules removed Hippolyta's golden girdle and tossed it to one of his men. "Put it in a safe place," he said, "many lives were lost to obtain it."

Hippolyta struggled in Hercules's grip. "You fought well," he said. "I want to take you with me as my own personal trophy."

She looked at him, horrified. "Do you think the queen of the Amazons would allow herself to become a souvenir?" She cried.

Hercules could feel his sympathy for a fallen warrior begin to take hold. Looking into her eyes he thought once again of the Ceryneian Hind, of how it was destined to remain untamed. This labor was quickly becoming the most challenging yet. He steeled his emotions and looked down in her face. He knew how it had to end.

"Oh, all prisoners of war say the same thing. But they all adapt!" said Hercules, forcing a cruel smile. "You'll become a prisoner of luxury at the palace. And don't worry, when Eurystheus tires of you, you can still find a good husband to give you that daughter. A shepherd, or maybe a farmer…a nice, quiet life."

Hippolyta became paler. "Kill me now—as a fellow warrior, I beg you to do it!" she pleaded. "Death in battle is the only honorable death for an Amazon."

"I know—that's why we're still fighting," whispered Hercules.

Hippolyta understood. Hercules knew that he was the only one who could offer Hippolyta an honorable exit. He held out the arm that held his sword, and Hippolyta threw herself onto it.

"Thank you," she whispered as the sword went through her.

Hercules's face was dark with anger and sadness. "That was the cruelest labor of them all," he said to Iolaus. "I've killed the greatest of warriors for the most miserable of kings!"

"You had no choice," said Iolaus quietly.

"We always have a choice," said Hercules.

SWEET DREAMS

Time passes for all mortals, but it was different for Hercules. The divine part of him allowed him to remain a man in the prime of his life as his friends grew older. His adventures had brought him fame and wealth, but he lived simply. Wherever his tent was pitched was where he called home.

He felt free and happy, most of the time. Sometimes he thought about Hippolyta, sometimes he listened too deeply to the love songs his friends sang around the campfire. It bothered him that Hera's hatred of him continued. Amphitryon and Alcmene had died, which left a great sadness within him. He felt lonely.

Lately, however, he had been dreaming of a girl. She visited his dreams every night and whispered words of love to him. When he awoke, he couldn't remember what she had said, but he felt less lonely.

He knew he was destined to meet this woman, sometime, somewhere. He kept his eyes open throughout his travels, but he never saw her. After a while he thought that maybe she didn't really exist, but he was still thankful for someone to keep him company in his dreams.

THE LAST LABORS

Hercules's tenth labor was to capture the Cattle of Geryon. Geryon was a monster with three heads and six arms.

It should come as no surprise that Hera stepped in to foil Hercules. Although he succeeded in this labor he was frustrated by how long he had been working on his labors. He was driven to cry out to Hera: "Why are you still against me, queen? Why will you not forgive me?"

Hera gave Hercules no answer. She sat on her throne and watched him in silence.

"Stop torturing him," whispered Aphrodite. "Why do you keep this up?"

Hera had no answer for her. The anger that had initially fueled her had dried up, her hatred of him had become less bitter.

The eleventh labor was to be the next to last task for Hercules. Hercules knew this, as did Eurystheus. The king was old now, and mad with jealousy at Hercules's eternal youth as well as his success at each of the impossible tasks he had been assigned. For the eleventh labor Hercules was to go into the Garden of the Hesperides and steal Hera's golden apples.

For the first time, Hercules tried to bargain with Eurystheus.

"Don't ask me to do this," said Hercules. "Hera hates me enough already!"

"Don't whine, Hercules, you're giving me a headache."

"Please, ask me to do anything else—I'll do it!"

"Your labors are not up for discussion," said Eurystheus. "Now get going."

THE GARDEN OF
THE HESPERIDES

Hercules asked Atlas for directions to the Garden of the Hesperides. Atlas spent much of his time alone, so the unexpected visit put the Titan in a good mood. He talked at length to Hercules, and warned him of potential dangers, such as the hundred-headed dragon named Ladon that guarded the garden.

Hercules walked for months before he reached his destination. When he arrived he couldn't believe his eyes. The Garden of the Hesperides

was delightful—the colors, scents, plants, and animals were all divinely beautiful. He found himself thinking that he would like to bring the girl who visited him in his dreams there.

It was dangerous to spend too much time dreaming. Soon enough, Ladon reared its ugly heads, and Hercules killed him. He gathered the apples and brought them back to Eurystheus.

"There you go!" barked Hercules, laying the apples before Eurystheus. "I'll allow you to enjoy them for a little while, but you must swear that you will return them to Hera, their rightful owner."

"I swear, I swear!" said Eurystheus.

Eurystheus did return the apples. He put on a sweet face and told Hera that it was his idea to return the apples to their queen, but of course Hera knew the truth. She looked at him sternly. This king was beginning to disgust her. She would teach him a lesson after the last labor was done.

HEBE'S LOVE

Aphrodite nudged Hebe. They were in the Garden of the Hesperides, watching Hera count and recount her golden apples.

"What?" asked Hebe.

"Be brave!" encouraged Aphrodite.

"Mother, I'd like to talk—" began Hebe.

"Now? Can't you see that I'm busy? It was a nice gesture for Hercules to have the apples returned, but I want to make sure they are all here and that none are damaged."

"About Hercules..." Hebe began again. "I wanted to tell you...um, that I'm in love!"

"Eight, nine, ten...Really? Well, that's good news. Finally! I mean, you're the goddess of youth, but still, it's time you should start having children. Anyway," Hera added icily, "you didn't need to bring your Auntie Aphrodite, although I suppose she thinks it's her business."

"Professional duty," said Aphrodite, cringing.

"Yeah, well, too bad I'm her mother and not you." Hera turned to Hebe, "So who's the lucky man?"

"Well, that's what I needed to talk to you about..." said Hebe, tearing up. She turned to Aphrodite. "I can't—let's go!"

Aphrodite squared her shoulders. Time to go to work. "Hebe, Hercules is a lucky man to be loved by you!"

Everyone was silent. An apple fell from the tree and went *splat* on the ground.

"WHAT?" yelled Hera, her eyes bulging.

"I love him!" sobbed Hebe.

"And you set them up?" Hera asked Aphrodite.

"No, my queen. Love happened on its own. Remember love? How it makes the heart pound?"

"My heart is pounding right now—because I've just learned that my daughter thinks she's in love with the man I hate more than anything!" shouted Hera.

"It's true, Mother! I love him! Ever since I first laid eyes on him."

"Shut up!" said Hera, stomping her foot.

"You don't know what love is," said Hebe, gathering her courage. "When Hercules succeeds at his final labor—and he will succeed—he will have earned his place on Mount Olympus and I will marry him."

Hera saw the determination in her daughter's eyes. It startled her.

"The heart wants what it wants," said Aphrodite, simply.

INTO THE UNDERWORLD

Eurystheus had a terrible toothache. He stared at Hercules with all the hatred he could muster.

"For the twelfth labor you will go to the underworld and bring back Cerberus, the three-headed guard dog that stands at the entrance." He dismissed Hercules with a wave of his hand.

This was to be the most challenging of all the labors. No one had ever returned from the underworld. Hercules had never been to a place so deathly silent. He had never seen a place so

dark. This was the realm of Hades,
Zeus's brother.

Athena and Hermes had accompanied
Hercules as far as the underground passage that
led to the underworld, but he had to complete
this labor alone. He walked a few steps, holding
his club in his hand. A silent river of souls
flowed along the ground in the darkness. He saw
the souls of the newly dead waiting for Charon,
the ferryman, to bring them before Hades to
be judged.

"What brings you here, Hercules," came a
voice from the darkness. It was Hades. "I know
you are used to just taking what you want, but
that won't work here. Let's make a deal:
Cerberus is yours only if you can subdue him
without weapons."

Hercules bowed his head in respect for the
god and his wishes. He felt the pull of the

underworld urging his soul to leave his body. He closed his eyes and saw the young woman from his dreams. "Hold on," she said. He opened his eyes and there was Persephone, standing behind Hades, quietly mouthing those same words.

INTO THE LIGHT

Cerberus was monstrous, but Hercules had dealt with plenty of monsters in his time. He stood firm as all three heads barked at him viciously. He looked at the souls that Cerberus was charged with keeping in the underworld. He recognized the faces of departed family and friends. He realized that Cerberus was their torturer, and that made him angry.

When Cerberus lunged at Hercules he withstood his bites. He used his bare hands to choke and subdue the beast. He dragged the unconscious Cerberus from the underworld. He

bound him with chains and handed him to
Hermes, who was waiting near the entrance to
the underworld. "Take it to Eurystheus," he said,
"I need to return to the underworld."

Why did Hercules return to the underworld?
There were several reasons. He wanted to
confront the memories he had spent much of his
life trying to forget. He wanted to say good-bye
to friends he had not gotten to say farewell to.
He hugged Alcmene and Amphitryon. He
waved to Hippolyta, who sat on her horse in
the distance.

One by one, the souls returned to their place
in the underworld. Once he was alone, Hercules
buried his face in his hands and wept. When he
raised his head, he felt that he had made peace
with his past and was ready to look toward
the future.

Hercules rushed back to the surface, eager to start his new life. The Sun on his skin had never felt as warm and sweet as it did the moment he emerged from the underworld. He closed his eyes to savor the moment. When he opened them again, the woman from his dreams was standing in front of him. She held out her hand to him.

"Your labors are done. Zeus is waiting to welcome you to Mount Olympus and to grant you immortality. I am Hebe, the goddess of youth. I will take you there."

The woman of his dreams hadn't been a dream after all! He eagerly took her hand and rose with her toward Mount Olympus. He was ready to begin his new life.

GUESTS AT THE HOTEL OLYMPUS

ALCMENE (alk-MEE-nee) mother of Hercules.

AMPHITRYON (am-fih-TRY-on) Alcmene's husband. Their child was Iphicles, the half-brother of Hercules.

APHRODITE (af-ruh-DY-tee) goddess of love and beauty. Aphrodite is the wife of Hephaestus, god of fire.

APOLLO (uh-PA-low) god of music and prophecy. He was the son of Zeus and Leto, and the twin brother of Artemis.

ARES (AIR-eez) god of bloodthirsty warfare. He was the of Zeus and Hera.

ATHENA (uh-THEE-nuh) goddess of wisdom and of heroic and strategic warfare. She was born from Zeus's head.

EILEITHYIA (ee-lee-THY-ee-a) goddess of childbirth. She was the daughter of Zeus and Hera.

EROS (EH-ros) god of lustful love. His arrows cause whomever they strike to fall in love. He is the son of Hermes and Aphrodite.

EURYSTHEUS (yur-IS-thee-us) the king who assigns the Twelve Labors to Hercules.

HADES (HAY-deez) god of the underworld.

HEBE (HEE-bee) goddess of youth. She was the daughter of Zeus and Hera, and the wife of Hercules.

HELIOS (HEE-lee-os) god of the sun. He is the son of the Titans Hyperion and Theia. He brings daylight by driving it across the sky in his golden chariot.

HERA (HERE-uh) wife of Zeus. Mother of Hephaestus, Ares, Hebe, Eris, and Eileithyia.

HERCULES (HER-kyuh-lees) the hero of the twelve labors. He was the son of Zeus and Alcmene.

HERMES (HER-meez) winged messenger of the gods. He was the son of Zeus and the Maia.

THE HESPERIDES (THE heh-SPUR-ih-deez) three nymphs who guard Hera's garden of golden apples.

HIPPOLYTA (hih-PAH-luh-tuh) queen of the Amazons. She is the daughter of Ares.

IOLAUS (eye-oh-LAY-us) Iphicles's son. He helped Hercules with some of his Twelve Labors.

IPHICLES (IH-fih-klees) son of Alcmene and Amphitryon and half-brother of Hercules.

PERSEPHONE (per-SEH-foh-nee) daughter of Demeter and Zeus.

THESEUS (THEE-see-us) king of Athens. He was famous as the person who killed the Minotaur.

ZEUS (ZOOS) king of gods. He was the brother and husband of Hera. He was the father of many gods and goddesses, as well as of many heroic mortals.

GLOSSARY

ALLIANCE (uh-LY-ants) An association to further a
common interest.

CASTANETS (kas-tuh-NETS) Small handheld
percussion instruments.

DESTINED (DES-tind) To have been determined beforehand.

DESTINY (DES-tin-ee) A predetermined course of events.

GIRDLE (GER-dul) A beltlike piece of clothing that is
wrapped around the waist.

HERO (HEER-oh) A person who is brave and has a
noble character.

HIND (HYND) A female deer.

ILLEGITIMATE (il-luh-JIH-tih-mit) In royal families
children that are not offspring of both the king and
the queen are considered illegitimate because they
cannot take over the throne.

IMMORTALITY (ih-mor-TAI-ih-tee) The state of being
immortal, or living forever.

MANURE (muh-NOO-ur) The solid waste of animals.

MORTALS (MOR-tulz) Human beings. Unlike gods, mortals die.

REALM (RELM) A kingdom or domain.

SUBDUE (sub-DOO) To bring under control by force.

SYMPATHY (SIM-puh-thee) To feel for something.

TROPHY (TRO-fee) Something gained or given to someone to recognize a victory.

UNDERWORLD (UN-dur-wurld) The place where the souls of the dead live.

WARRIOR (WAR-yur) A person who fights in a war.

INDEX

FOR MORE INFORMATION

Books

Bryant, Megan E. *Oh My Gods!: A Look-It-Up Guide to the Gods of Mythology*. Danbury, Conn.: Franklin Watts, 2009.

Levine, Michelle. *The Greeks: Life in Ancient Greece*. Minneapolis: Millbrook Press, 2009.

Whiting, Jim. *Hercules*. Hockessin, DE: Mitchell Lane Publishers, 2007.

Web Sites

To ensure the currency and safety of recommended Internet links, Windmill maintains and updates an online list of sites related to the subject of this book. To access this list of Web sites, please go to www.windmillbooks.com/weblinks and select this book's title.

FOR MORE GREAT FICTION AND NONFICTION GO TO WINDMILLBOOKS.COM.